DRUGS AND MUSIC

Elvis Presley was killed by his amphetamine use.

THE DRUG ABUSE PREVENTION LIBRARY

DRUGS AND MUSIC

Carlienne Frisch

THE ROSEN PUBLISHING GROUP, INC.

NEW YORK

The people pictured in this book are only models; they in no way practice or endorse the activities illustrated. Captions serve only to explain the subjects of photographs and do not in any way imply a connection between the real-life models and the staged situations shown.

Published in 1995 by The Rosen Publishing Group, Inc.
29 East 21st Street, New York, NY 10010

First Edition

Library of Congress Cataloging-in-Publication Data

Frisch, Carlienne, 1944–
    Drugs and music / Carlienne Frisch.
        p.   cm. — (The Drug abuse prevention library)
    Includes bibliographical references and index.
    ISBN 0-8239-1707-X
        1. Drug abuse—Juvenile literature.   2. Musicians—
    Drug use—Juvenile literature.   3. Drug abuse—
    Prevention—Juvenile literature.   4. Drugs and
    popular music—Juvenile literature.   [1. Drug abuse.
    2. Musicians—Drug use.   3. Drugs and popular
    music].   I. Title.   II. Series.
    HV5809.5.F75   1994
    364.1′77′08878—dc20   94-1026
                                                                                    CIP
                                                                                     AC

Manufactured in the United States of America

Contents

Introduction

*S*am *is watching out for Karen. He opens
the door before she even knocks and says,*
"Hi, Karen, let's party!"

*Karen hears an Eric Clapton tape
blaring from the basement—*"If you wanna
hang out, you've gotta take her out,
cocaine . . ." *Karen goes down to the
entertainment room. Lisa and Juan are
already there. Juan pops open a can of beer
and hands it to Karen.*

"Hey, Karen, want a joint?" *Lisa holds
out a marijuana cigarette. Karen shakes her
head. She's beginning to be sorry she came.
She's worried about her friends' behavior,
and she wonders what kinds of drugs Lisa
has with her. Karen hopes this evening won't
turn out like the party last week, when Juan*

threw up all over the couch and Lisa just sat and cried.

"What's going to happen if we get caught with this stuff?" Karen asks. "Even if we don't get caught, getting high could make us sick and even kill us."

"Hey, be cool," Sam says. "Lots of rock stars get high. And they say it's OK."

"Yeah, I know," Karen says. "I've read that the Beatles used marijuana and LSD. "In the '60s, a lot of people took drugs, and a lot of people died from overdoses or bad drugs."

There have always been people who thought that drugs and music go together. But knowledgeable musicians know that drugs interfere with their art form, and with their energy, so they avoid drugs.

This book will help you understand why drugs are dangerous. You will find out how the lyrics (words) of some songs could make some people want to use drugs. You will understand how to enjoy music for its own sake. Drugs only make it harder to be truly aware of what's going on. They actually dull the senses.

Jimi Hendrix died of a drug overdose when he was only
27 years old.

CHAPTER 1

What Are Drugs and What Is Addiction?

First, let's take a look at drugs and drug addiction. A drug is a chemical that changes the way you feel or think or behave.

People who use drugs lose control of their feelings, thoughts, and actions. Most people who use drugs become addicted, or hooked. These people are called drug addicts. People who are addicted to alcohol are called alcoholics.

Once a person is hooked, he or she wants to keep using drugs, no matter what. The addict loses concern for his or her own well-being, and also for other people. Addicts will do anything to get drugs.

Legal Drugs

10 | Medicines are legal drugs, and some of them can be bought over the counter. Others require a doctor's written order, called a prescription.

Caffeine is a drug that exists naturally in coffee and tea. Caffeine is also added to colas. It is a stimulant that raises blood pressure and causes the stomach to produce more acid.

People want caffeine because it makes them feel alert and full of energy. But caffeine can make people nervous or keep them from being able to sleep at night.

If you drink caffeine often, you develop a tolerance for it. That means you need more caffeine to get the same feelings of energy and alertness.

When caffeine addicts do not get enough caffeine, they may feel tired and sleepy. Some people get headaches when they do not have caffeine.

Illegal Drugs

Some drugs are illegal for teenagers to use. It is illegal to sell tobacco to anyone under 18 years of age. For people under age 21, it is illegal to purchase alcohol or to drink alcohol anywhere except at home.

Alcohol includes beer, wine, and hard liquor such as gin, vodka, whiskey, and brandy.

Some drugs are so dangerous that it has been made illegal for anyone to have them. These drugs include marijuana, cocaine, crack, hallucinogens, and heroin.

Tobacco

Tobacco and tobacco smoke are harmful to our health. But many people smoke pipes, cigars, or cigarettes. A million teen-agers and children in the United States start smoking cigarettes every year. Some also chew tobacco and use snuff, tobacco that is breathed in through the nose.

Tobacco contains nicotine and tar, two harmful substances. Nicotine is habit-forming. It also injures the lungs, throat, blood, and other organs. It travels from the lungs into the bloodstream very quickly. It speeds up the nervous system and the heart. At the same time, nicotine reduces the amount of blood that reaches the heart.

Tar is a very complex cancer-causing chemical. Carbon monoxide, a poisonous gas, is also found in tobacco smoke. Most cigarette smokers develop diseases of the lungs. Many develop cancer.

12 | *Alcohol*

Karen knows that she and her friends shouldn't drink alcohol. But last week, Mark brought some 12-packs of beer to Sam's house. Mark's older brother had bought them for him. Karen and Sam both drank several cans of beer. Karen felt relaxed and happy as she and Sam danced together. The music was hot, and Sam was a good dancer.

But after a while Sam started to disagree with everything Karen said. His voice got louder and louder. He grabbed Karen's arm so hard it hurt and yelled that she was stupid. As soon as he let go of her, Karen left the party.

Three people die every hour because of drunk drivers. Every year, alcohol kills about 50,000 Americans in auto accidents. Almost as many people die each year from other problems caused by alcohol. Alcohol is the major drug problem of American teens.

At first, alcohol makes people feel relaxed. They get a pleasant feeling called a *high*. But then they begin to lose self-control. Alcohol is a depressant that travels quickly through the bloodstream to the brain. There, the alcohol depresses, or slows down, the central nervous system.

Jim Morrison of the Doors heavily abused drugs until
his death.

14 This means a loss of some control over body and speech.

Alcohol also slows muscle movements. Many people who use alcohol cannot think clearly. They take unnecessary risks like driving too fast. Some people get angry and say or do things they regret later.

Alcohol can damage the liver, kidneys, heart, and stomach. It can also cause diarrhea and skin problems.

Just one drink can result in a hangover (a pounding headache), or make a person throw up. Just one drink can make a person unsteady. Just one drink can blur thinking and cause people to do something they know is wrong. Just one drink can cause a person to have an auto accident.

Amphetamines

Amphetamines have many names. They are called "speed," "uppers," "pep pills," "bennies," "whites," "exies," "meth," "crystal," and "crank." Amphetamines speed up the central nervous system.

On Friday evening, Karen and Jana went to a dance club that didn't serve alcohol. Jana danced to every song, even when she didn't have a partner. She made up steps as she went along.

When the deejay took a break, Jana took a white pill out of her purse and handed it to Karen.

"Here, this will get you going," Jana said. "It's Dexedrine—a diet pill—an 'upper.' My mom has a prescription to help her lose weight. I take them to give me extra energy."

Karen shook her head and pushed the pill away.

"No, my sister did what you're doing, and she got hooked," she said.

Amphetamines can make people become so active that they push their bodies to exhaustion.

Many users develop a tolerance to amphetamines. This tolerance is both physical and psychological. At first, the person feels alert and self-confident. But when those good feelings end, the person becomes depressed and wants more amphetamines. The user is hooked.

Some people who abuse amphetamines don't eat enough and become sick from malnutrition.

People hooked on amphetamines need a doctor's help. Trying to stop without a doctor's help can lead to deep depression or even suicide.

16 | *Depressants*

Depressants have the opposite effect on the body. They are called "downers" because they slow the central nervous system. They slow the heart rate and the breathing. They lower blood pressure.

The three kinds of depressants are barbiturates, tranquilizers, and methaqualone. Barbiturates are called "barbs," "goof balls," and "blues." Other names for methaqualone are "soapers," "quads," and "ludes."

Barbiturates can cause confusion. People have less control over their feelings. Their reactions are slower, and they seem to be intoxicated. This makes it dangerous to drive a car or operate machinery.

Tranquilizers relax the body. They can also cause sleepiness, confusion, and loss of control over the muscles.

Depressants can cause physical and psychological dependence. Users develop a tolerance and need larger and larger amounts to get the same effect.

Some people take a depressant and then drink alcohol. This can result quickly in coma and death.

Alcohol is the major drug problem for American teens.

Prescription drugs should never be taken without consulting a doctor.

Marijuana

Marijuana is made from the dried leaves and flowers of a plant called *Cannabis sativa*. The main chemical in marijuana is *tetrahydrocannabinol,* or THC. It is also called "grass," "pot," "weed," and "maryjane." A marijuana cigarette is called a *joint* or *reefer*.

A marijuana user feels relaxed and silly at first, then sleepy. Marijuana increases the pulse rate, lowers body temperature, slows muscle movements, and affects one's sense of timing. That makes it dangerous to drive after smoking pot.

A pot smoker feels "high" for just a

Chronic use of marijuana can cause the user to lose interest in life.

few hours, but it takes as long as a month for marijuana to leave the body.

The more THC there is in a marijuana cigarette, the more harmful it is to the body. A person who uses marijuana over a long time may develop a physical tolerance to the drug. But there is even more danger that a pot smoker will develop a psychological need and will lose interest in healthy and pleasurable activities.

Cocaine and Crack
Cocaine is made from the leaves of the coca plant. It is also called "coke,"

20 "snow," and "flake." Cocaine is usually made into a fine, white powder. Crack, also called "rock," is a very potent form of cocaine. Crack is made into large, white crystals.

A cocaine user snorts, or sniffs, the powder into the nose. Some users inject, or shoot, cocaine into a vein with a hypodermic needle. Users begin to feel restless, overconfident, and alert. But some become confused, anxious, and depressed. They feel paranoid, thinking that other people are out to get them. Heavy doses of cocaine can cause a person to have hallucinations, or to see, hear, or feel things that aren't really there.

Crack is smoked or freebased. The user feels a very strong high that lasts five or ten minutes. Then a very strong crash, or feeling of withdrawal, follows. The user feels tired, anxious, and depressed. After trying crack only once or twice, a person is usually hooked.

The body reacts to cocaine and crack in the same ways, but crack's effects are faster. The heartbeat speeds up greatly, and one is in danger of having a heart attack. The blood pressure rises. The brain receives less oxygen, which can cause a stroke. The pupils of the eyes

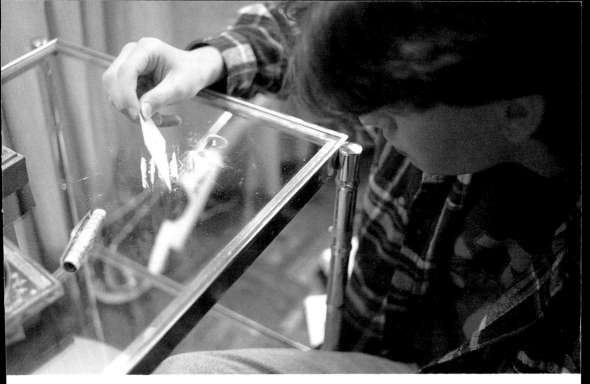

The effects of cocaine are extremely unpredictable.

dilate. People have hallucinations and paranoia.

The effects of cocaine are unpredictable. Cocaine can cause convulsions and death. Some people can use cocaine or crack for a while without having a bad reaction. But some people die after only one dose.

Hallucinogens

Some hallucinogens are made from plants. Others are synthetic drugs, made in a chemical laboratory. Hallucinogens are "mind-benders." They cause changes in perception, or how one sees and understands one's surroundings. Users

Hallucinogens can cause the user to lose muscle control.

feel that they have left their bodies and are seeing and hearing "magical" things.

Throughout history, certain groups of people have used natural hallucinogens such as mushrooms and peyote cactus buttons in religious ceremonies and rituals. The natural hallucinogens cause users to see brilliant colors that are not really there and to lose track of time and space. But they can also make people feel ill. They can cause fast changes in mood, and also depression.

One of the synthetic hallucinogens is lysergic acid diethylamide, usually called LSD or acid. It is a very dangerous drug.

LSD increases heart rate, blood pressure, and the amount of sugar in the blood. It makes the breathing irregular. An LSD user often has a strong feeling that everything is wonderful. The person cannot separate fact from fantasy. Some users are killed because they think they can fly from high buildings or stop trains by putting their hands out.

The LSD user may also panic or become paranoid. Some become violent and hurt themselves or the people around them. Users quickly develop a tolerance to the drug.

LSD can still affect people after they

24 | stop using it. Some users have "flash-backs" days or weeks later, reliving the experience.

Another very dangerous synthetic hallucinogen is phencyclidine. It is also called PCP or "angel dust."

PCP users usually inject, or shoot, the drug into a vein. The effects are similar to those of LSD. PCP users quickly develop a tolerance to the drug. They may become violent.

Heroin

Heroin, also called "horse," is a white powder made from opium, which is a drug that comes from poppy plants. Heroin users, called junkies, inject or inhale the drug. They often use infected hypodermic needles that someone else has used. They may catch AIDS, hepatitis, and other horrible diseases.

A heroin user has a slower heart rate and shallow breathing, feels restless, drowsy, or nauseated. Heroin gives the user a powerful high followed by a feeling of relaxation. Then comes a crash, with painful cramps, diarrhea, chills, or sweating for a week or more.

It is illegal for people under 21 to purchase alcohol.

CHAPTER 2

Out of Tune— Musicians and Drugs

Many people have become drug addicts or alcoholics because they used drugs when they listened to music or were a part of the music world. To these people, drugs and music seem to go together, like popcorn and movies.

Music has always been part of human life. Before there was writing, young people learned the history and rules of their culture through ceremonies and rituals that included playing musical instruments, singing, and dancing.

In some ceremonies hallucinogenic plants were used. Often, the religious leader was the only person who used drugs. Sometimes, though, young people were given drugs as part of the coming of age ceremony. But drugs were not something to be used in everyday life. They were only for sacred ceremonies.

Some of Karen's friends have started using drugs because they think it makes them seem grown up. It also makes them feel wanted, as part of a group. Karen is afraid that if she says no to her friends' drugs, they won't want to be with her. But Karen doesn't want to use drugs.

Karen decides to talk to her school counselor, Mr. Wang. "Many young people have problems with drugs," Mr. Wang tells Karen. "Getting together and listening to music affects the emotions. The rhythm can be exciting. It makes people want to move in time with the music. And the lyrics in some songs even tell people to use drugs."

Karen nods and says, "Like the Grateful Dead lyrics— 'Take a vacation, fall out for a while. Summer's comin' in, and it's goin' outa style. Well, lie down smokin', honey; have yourself a ball . . .' *Isn't that telling us to smoke marijuana?"*

"Yes, but there are also lyrics that tell you drugs are no good," Mr. Wang answers. "My son told me about MC Lyte's rap against drug use. The rapper is shocked that 'the girl you was addicted to, her name was crack.'

28

"Music can change your emotions. And your friends can affect your emotions. But how you act on your feelings is up to you. When the people around you are using drugs, you can make the choice not to use drugs."

Karen thanks Mr. Wang. She decides to tell her friends that she wants to party with them, but she does not want to use any drugs, not even alcohol.

Young people have always been tempted to use drugs and alcohol. Wherever they have gotten together to listen or dance to jazz, country music, rock and roll, soul, hard rock or rap, some of them have used drugs.

Many young musicians have died because of drug use. Some of your favorite rappers or MTV stars may be addicted to alcohol and other drugs. You can enjoy the beauty of their music and their art without copying their bad habits.

Drug use is not a new problem for musicians. Many of them have to travel constantly and perform in different cities every night. They have no permanent home. They are lonely. The other musicians become their family, and if they are taking drugs it is hard to resist joining them. It is easy to get drugs from other musicians or from drug sellers (pushers).

Let's take a look at how drugs have caused problems for musicians.

The Classical Era

Johann Sebastian Bach was addicted to caffeine. He even wrote a short choral song about coffee. Bach was a composer who was born in Germany about 300 years ago.

Ludwig van Beethoven was also addicted to coffee. When Beethoven was young, more than 200 years ago, his father would bring friends home from bars in the middle of the night. Beethoven had to get up from a sound sleep and play for them. He may have taken to coffee to stay awake.

Johannes Brahms was a teenager in Hamburg, Germany, about 150 years ago. To help support his family, Brahms played dance music in the bars on the waterfront. The bartenders gave Brahms free drinks. He later became a composer of classical music, but his drinking didn't stop.

Stephen Foster wrote his first song at age 13. When he was 21, his *Oh! Susanna* was the most popular song in the United States. Foster wrote more than 200 songs. He spent much of the money he made

Ludwig van Beethoven was addicted to caffeine.

from them to buy alcohol. He would often write a song in the morning, sell it in the afternoon, and spend the money in bars in the evening. He died at age 38.

All That Jazz

The 1920s and 1930s were called the Jazz Era. They were also the Prohibition Era. Making or selling alcoholic beverages was prohibited (illegal) in the United States. But some people made alcohol at home. They called it "bathtub gin" or "white lightning." Some of the alcohol was of such poor quality that it poisoned and even killed the people who drank it.

Every so often, the teenagers of that era heard on the radio or read in the newspaper that a jazz musician had died from using drugs. Some performers received drugs instead of money for their performances.

Some musicians think alcohol or other drugs help them perform better. But they are wrong. Drugs damage the ability to make music. Bix Beiderbecke found that out.

By the time Bix was 20, he was a well-known jazz musician. He played the piano and the cornet. Bix became an alcoholic. Drinking ended his musical

32 | career and his life. Bix was 28 years old when he died of alcoholism and pneumonia.

In 1931, Billie Holiday was 15 years old. She was already singing the blues and jazz in bars. Billie married a heroin addict, who shared the drug with her. Soon, Billie was hooked. By the early 1940s, she was spending $1,000 a week on heroin.

Billie tried to get over her addiction, but she didn't succeed. She was arrested for possession of narcotics and sent to jail. When she got out of jail, she had a hard time getting a job. She said, "If you think dope is for kicks and for thrills, you're out of your mind. If you think you need stuff [drugs] to play music or sing, you're crazy. It can fix you so you can't play nothing or sing nothing."

Country and Western

The lyrics of some country and western songs say that alcohol will help people get through an unhappy time. Some songs even make people feel unhappy. It is important to remember that you can make choices that are good for you. You should choose to stay away from

Billie Holliday tried for years to get over her heroin addiction, but never succeeded.

34 | alcohol and other drugs when you are
unhappy.

Country singer Hank Williams made
bad choices. Hank sang songs like "I'm
So Lonesome I Could Cry" and "Your
Cheating Heart." The songs showed
how Hank felt about his life. He tried
to escape his problems by using alcohol
and other drugs. That continued even
after he became a big success in 1948,
when he was 25. Hank's band members
tried to keep him from drinking.

Then Hank hurt his back, and his doctor prescribed medicine to control the
pain. Hank also had pills to help him
relax. One day he took both medicines
and probably drank some alcohol. A few
hours later, Hank's driver found him
dead on the back seat of his car. Hank
was 29 years old.

Johnny Cash, another famous country
singer, had drug problems, too. Johnny
was a successful performer at age 25,
but he felt tired and overworked. One
night, Johnny was afraid he might fall
asleep while driving all night to the next
concert. He got a "pep pill" (amphetamine) from another musician in the car.
Johnny took another one before he went
on stage. Soon, he was taking ampheta-

mines every day. Then he used alcohol and barbiturates to help him sleep. He was addicted to both "uppers" and "downers."

Finally, Johnny was taking nearly 100 pills a day. He went to Mexico where he could buy 1,000 pills without a prescription. The police were watching, and Johnny was arrested when he came back into the United States.

Johnny's addiction was hurting his career and his health. He finally got help, and overcame his addiction.

Rock and Roll

Girls and boys gathered at the local hamburger drive-in. It was 1957, and their car radios were tuned to the latest music— rock and roll. At home, they danced to Elvis Presley's "Heartbreak Hotel" or Jerry Lee Lewis' hit, "Whole Lot of Shakin' Going On."

"Whole Lot of Shakin' " describes much of Jerry's life. At 16, he married a preacher's daughter and did some preaching himself. The marriage lasted about a year, and from that time on, Jerry's life went downhill. In the next few years, Jerry played piano and sang in truck stops. Some of the drivers

Jerry Lee Lewis was one of the first rock musicians.

took amphetamines to stay awake so
they could drive all night. They often
tipped Jerry with amphetamines. It
was the start of a lifelong problem for
him.

As his singing career took off, Jerry got
married several more times, sometimes
without bothering to get divorced first.
Soon, Jerry had several hit songs, but his
personal problems kept him from going
on major concert tours. He tried to make
himself feel better by drinking bourbon
and taking Benzedrine.

Jerry's drug use damaged his health. In
1976, when he entered a hospital to have
his gall bladder removed, the doctors also
treated him for a collapsed lung and for a
lung disease called pleurisy.

In 1979 and 1980 he was arrested for
possession of drugs. In 1983, his fifth
wife, Shawn Stevens, died of a drug overdose. Jerry confessed in 1988 that he had
spent $500,000 on Demerol, an addictive
painkiller. He described his life in these
words: "Jerry Lee Lewis is not an all-
American hero story."

Elvis Presley became a legend in his
own time—the King of Rock and Roll.
But neither fame nor wealth protected
Elvis from the dangers of drug abuse.

38   Elvis first took amphetamines when he was in the army. When he got out of the army, he got amphetamines prescribed by a doctor. Elvis thought the "uppers" made him perform better and helped with the depression after his mother's death. Like Johnny Cash, Elvis began taking barbiturates to help him relax and sleep.

Elvis' unhealthy way of life caused him to feel ill. So, his doctors prescribed pain-killers and sedatives. Elvis was able to convince himself he wasn't a drug abuser because his pills were prescription medicines. When Elvis went on a concert tour, his suitcases were loaded with dozens of little bottles of pills.

Elvis continued to use drugs and over-eat. He got fatter, his heart was enlarged, his colon was twisted, and his liver was damaged. Some of his concert tours had to be canceled because of his poor health.

The week before he died, Elvis filled prescriptions for 278 tablets of Dexedrine and Biphetamine. He also got 262 tablets of Amytal and Quaalude, 150 tablets of Percodan, and 20 cubic centimeters of Dilaudid.

On August 16, 1977, Elvis was found

Jerry Lee Lewis described his life as "not an all-American hero story."

Woodstock was a huge music festival in 1969 that defined a generation.

slumped on his bathroom floor. He was dead when he reached the hospital. Doctors said the immediate cause of death was a damaged heart.

The Sixties

The 1960s were a time of conflict between generations. Many students and other young people believed that their parents' generation put too much value on money and power. The young people wanted a world where peace and love were more important. They wanted the United States to stop fighting in the Vietnam War in Asia, which they thought was unjust.

Many young people lost confidence in the government when several of their heroes were murdered by assassins. In 1963, President John F. Kennedy was killed by a shot in the head. The African-American leader Malcolm X was killed in 1965. African-American leader Martin Luther King, Jr., and Senator Robert Kennedy (John Kennedy's brother) were both assassinated in 1968. All across the country, disillusioned young people protested on college campuses and at political conventions.

42   Many young people dropped out of their parents' culture. Some lived in communes, in which they shared houses, food, and drugs. They thought using drugs would help them understand themselves and the world. Musicians sang about love, peace, understanding—and drugs.

In the 1960s, many musicians used drugs, especially amphetamines. Being "freaky" and strange was "in." Some of the 1960s music was written for people to listen to while on drugs. The musical group Velvet Underground had a song named "Heroin." Some people thought Peter, Paul and Mary's hit "Puff, the Magic Dragon" was about smoking drugs.

The Simon and Garfunkel song "Bridge Over Troubled Waters" is still popular today. Many of the words suggest drug use. "Silver girl" is slang for a hypodermic needle. The line "Your time has come to shine" suggests a drug trip. "If you need a friend, I am sailing just behind" means the pusher is always there with more drugs.

In August 1969, about a half million young people went to the Woodstock Music and Art Fair, a three-day concert

The Beatles eventually stopped using drugs.

on a farm in New York State. There were so many drugs that people later said, "If you can remember being at Woodstock, you weren't *really* at Woodstock."

Stars of the 1960s

In 1963, The Beatles came to the United States from England. The Beatles—John Lennon, Paul McCartney, George Harrison, and Ringo Starr—soon became world-famous. The Beatles used marijuana, amphetamines, and LSD. The ini-

Boys II Men is a completely clean R&B group.

tials of the their song "Lucy in the Sky with Diamonds" stand for LSD. Eventually, the Beatles learned that drugs would not help them understand themselves or the world, and they stopped using drugs.

Soul singer James Brown also smoked marijuana. He began lacing, or adding to, his reefers with PCP and became addicted to it. The PCP caused him to act irresponsibly. He was sent to prison for

possession of PCP, carrying a pistol, and

trying to outrun the police in a high-speed car chase.

Many musicians were arrested for drug possession in the 1960s, and some died from drug overdoses. Mick Jagger, Keith Richard, and Brian Jones of the Rolling Stones all had legal problems that involved drugs. When Jones drowned in 1969, he had been using alcohol, amphetamines, and barbiturates.

Rock singer Jimi Hendrix died of an overdose of barbiturates in 1970. A few weeks later, rock singer Janis Joplin died from a combination of heroin, alcohol, and Valium.

The mystery of rock singer Jim Morrison's death in 1971 has never been solved. Jim was known for his drug use and his drinking. At the age of 27, he died while taking a bath. Jim's wife, Pamela, and a doctor agreed that Jim had died of a heart attack, not a drug overdose. But Jim's body was buried before anyone else saw it. Pamela died four years later of a heroin overdose.

River Phoenix was known for his cleancut reputation. He was a vegetarian and a crusader for animal rights, a supporter of Amnesty International, and was very vocal in his belief that the environ-

46 | ment needed protection. His unexpected
death in October of 1993 shocked the
world. The actor most fans thought was
completely clean had overdosed on heroin
and cocaine. The world had lost another
talented actor to drugs.

Kurt Cobain, the lead singer of
Nirvana, had a long-standing love-hate
relationship with heroin. With his wife
Courtney Love and his baby girl Francis
Bean, he seemed to be coming out from
under the shadow of drugs. However, all
was not as it seemed: Kurt's overdose in
Rome prompted Courtney to insist he get
professional help for his problem. He
entered a rehabilitation center, only to
leave a week later without telling family
or friends where he was. His electrician
finally found him. He had taken heroin
and then blown his brains out with a
shotgun, leaving behind a devastated
Courtney and an orphaned Francis Bean.

Some Who Got Free
Many musicians learned from their mis-
takes and stopped taking drugs. Many
went to doctors for help. Eric Clapton,
Boy George, and Peter Townshend of
the rock group The Who are just a few
examples.

Members of the rock band Aerosmith also gave up using drugs and alcohol. Band member Steven Tyler said, "I was a garbage head—heroin, coke, Valium, anything . . ." Joe Perry could scarcely wait for a performance to end so he could go backstage and take drugs. Joe explained, "We didn't do it for escape. We were addicted."

The motto of the Beastie Boys was "Let's party!" Their rap lyrics were about "beer drinkin', breath stinkin', sniffin' glue." Then, the Beastie Boys dropped out of the music scene for a few years. When they returned in 1992, they weren't party boys anymore. Their image was "clean."

The new urban soul group Boys II Men is completely clean, and, in fact, that is the lifestyle they promote.

Dave Mustaine, the lead singer with the heavy metal band Megadeth, used heroin, cocaine, amphetamines, and alcohol. In 1990, he was arrested for having drugs in his car. He was given a choice of going to jail or to a drug treatment program. Dave got clean and found he was a better musician when sober.

CHAPTER 3

Staying in Tune— and Off Drugs

*D*o you walk the same way each time you go to a friend's house? Do you sit in the same seat at the movies each time? When we do the same things in the same way every time, we develop habits. When we feel we *should* always do the same things in the same way, we have created a ritual.

Some habits and rituals are good, such as brushing teeth after every meal. Some habits and rituals are harmful, such as smoking a cigarette after each meal. A ritual that includes using drugs is very harmful.

Every Friday evening, Andy and Jennie meet Tom and Laura at the mall to play video games. Later, they go to Laura's

house, where they listen to music, eat snacks,
*and drink beer. No one else is home. Tom
lights a marijuana joint and passes it around.
The couples close their eyes and dance.*

*Jennie is uncomfortable. She does not
want to smoke or drink. Her brother is an
alcoholic, and she does not want to get
hooked too. Jennie is also worried that Andy
might already be an alcoholic. One evening,
as the group is leaving the mall, Jennie suggests going to her house instead of Laura's.*

"You got any beer?" Andy asks.

"We don't have *to have beer," Jennie
replies.*

*"Hey, what's a Friday night without
beer!" Andy says. The beer and the music
are part of a ritual that makes Andy feel
accepted by his friends.*

*Jennie turns to Andy. "Why do you
always want to get drunk?"*

"Hey, it's tradition," Andy says.

*"Well, count me out," Jennie says. "Beer
makes me feel sick. And we could get into
trouble."*

*"Hey, that hasn't happened yet," Andy
says. "Come on, Jennie, what's wrong with
you tonight?" He sounds hurt and angry.*

*"It's hard to explain," Jennie says. "But
let's do something different, like check out the
new juice bar on State Street."*

Drinking while listening to music can become a habit. It's up to you to break the habit.

Andy starts to shake his head, but Tom says, "That's cool," and Laura agrees. Andy shrugs and goes along with his friends. Jennie is looking forward to an evening of fun and music without having to worry about drugs.

Music and drugs can easily become part of a ritual. Some people, like Jason, have a solitary ritual that does not include friends.

Jason's friends are the rock bands he listens to. Sometimes it seems to him that

marijuana is his friend, too. Jason spends

most of his evenings in his room, smoking a reefer and listening to heavy metal.

Jason's mother is worried about him, but she does not know what to say to him about drugs. She asks her friend, Bill Riley, to talk with Jason. Bill is a former user. He agrees to try to help Jason and invites him to a baseball game. They stop for pizza after the game, and Bill tells Jason about his own problems with drugs.

"A few years ago, my girlfriend broke up with me about the same time I lost my job and wrecked my car," Bill tells Jason. "I was in major pain. I made the mistake of thinking drugs would make my problems go away. But I was just making more problems for myself."

"What kind of problems?" Jason asks.

"I had to get money to buy the drugs," Bill says. "And I was always afraid the police would catch me making the buy. But I kept on because I wanted to get high. Then I did not feel so lonely and unhappy."

"Why did you quit?" Jason asks.

Bill smiles. "My sister was worried about me. She got me into a drug treatment program. The counselor taught me that I could change my habits and my attitude. I started listening to tapes that made me feel good, and I coached a basketball team at the

YMCA. Some of the guys on the team are my friends now."

Bill's advice helped Jason. If you or one of your friends are using drugs to try to escape your problems, you can get help, too. Find out if students meet in a group in your community to discuss their problems and interests. If not, you may be able to start such a support group. You can also call one of the agencies in the Help List.

If you have used drugs while listening to music, there are questions you can ask yourself that will help you make better choices. Ask yourself if the music makes you feel good or bad. Ask yourself if the lyrics or the music make you want to do things you don't do otherwise. Ask yourself if the music and the lyrics match up with your own values and attitudes. When you have answered the questions, you will be able to decide if the music and lyrics you listen to are a good choice.

You can buy tapes or records that do not promote drug use. A national group called the Parents Music Resource Center encourages music companies to print lyrics or a warning on albums. You can watch out for the warning that says "Explicit Lyrics" or for albums that have

Smoking pot can alienate you from the rest of the world.

Some lyrics are labeled "explicit."

the lyrics printed on them. You can choose tapes or records that do not mention drugs.

You may be in favor of labeling music. Your parents may be pleased that the rap or rock tapes you buy do not promote drugs. Or you may think it is wrong to put labels on records and tapes. You may be concerned that singers will censor their lyrics because of the labeling. If you are in favor of labeling music, you may want to contact the Parents Music Resource Center, which is listed in the back of this book. If you think music should not be labeled, you may contact the American Civil Liberties Union, which is also listed. The Help List also gives the phone numbers and addresses of places where you can get help if you need it.

If you are drug-free, you have made a very important, good choice in your life. But if you are using tobacco, alcohol, or other drugs, it is not too late to change your behavior.

Help List

Write or Call:
Drug Abuse Hot Line:
Call 1-800-662-HELP (4357)

Cocaine Hot Line:
Call 1-800-COCAINE (262-2463)

**Alcohol and Drug Dependence Help
   Line:**
Call 1-800-622-2255

Students to Offset Peer Pressure
P.O. Box 103, Department S
Hudson, NH 03051-0103

SADD (Students Against Drunk Driving)
Box 800
Marlboro, MA 01752

Narcotics Anonymous
World Service Office
16155 Wyandotte Street
Van Nuys, CA 91406

Al-Anon or Alateen
P.O. Box 862
Midtown Station
New York, NY 10018-0862

National Clearinghouse for Alcohol and Drug Information
P.O. Box 2345
Rockville, MD 20852

Canada

Alcohol and Drug Dependency Information and counseling Services (ADDICS)
#2, 24711/2 Portage Avenue
Winnipeg, MB R3J 0N6
204-831-1999

Alcoholics Anonymous, Toronto
#502, Intergroup Office
234 Englinton Avenue E.
Toronto, ON M4P 1K5
416-487-5591

Narcotics Anonymous
P.O. Box 7500
Station A
Toronto, ON M5W 1P9
416-691-9519

In Your Telephone Book: In the Yellow Pages, look under Alcoholism, Drug Abuse, Counselors. In the business section of the White Pages, in the back of the book, look for Alcoholics Anonymous, Al-Anon, Narcotics Anonymous, National Council of Alcoholism, and Cocaine Anonymous.

58 Under Government Listings, in the front of the book, look for Alcoholism Treatment, Drug Abuse, and County Health Services.

At School: Check the bulletin boards in your school counseling office or nurse's office for TEEN HOT LINES in your town.

To find out about labels on records and tapes:
Parents Music Resource Center
1500 Arlington Boulevard
Arlington, VA 22209
(703) 527-9466

American Civil Liberties Union
132 West 43rd Street
New York, NY 10036
(212) 944-9800

Glossary
Explaining New Words

acid   Street name for the hallucinogen lysergic acid diethylamide (LSD).

addict   Person who has a physical or psychological need for a habit-forming drug.

addiction   Physical or psychological need for a habit-forming drug.

addictive   Habit-forming.

alcoholic   Person who is addicted to alcohol.

amphetamines   Prescription medications that speed up the central nervous system.

angel dust   Street name for the hallucinogen phencyclidine, also called PCP.

barbiturates   Prescription medications that slow down the central nervous system.

caffeine   Chemical in colas, coffee, and tea that stimulates the body.

Cannabis sativa   The plant from which marijuana is obtained.

60 | **carbon monoxide**   Colorless, poisonous gas formed when carbon is not completely burned.

central nervous system   The brain and spinal cord, which receive messages from the outside world and send messages to the muscles of the body.

cocaine   Powerful stimulant of the central nervous system.

coke   Street name for cocaine.

crash   The physical and mental depression that follows a drug high.

depressants   Drugs that slow down the central nervous system.

depression   Feeling of deep sadness; feeling "down."

drug   Chemical substance that changes the way the mind or body works.

flashback   Repetition of a drug experience, sometimes long after the drug was used.

hallucinations   Seeing, hearing, or feeling things that are not there.

hallucinogens   Drugs that cause hallucinations and changes in how you see and understand your surroundings.

hangover   Strong headache usually caused by drinking alcohol.

high   Affected by alcohol or drugs.

hooked Being addicted to alcohol or
other drugs.

lysergic acid diethylamide (LSD)
Hallucinogen that is made in a chemical laboratory.

nicotine Colorless, poisonous, habit-forming chemical in cigarettes.

paranoia Feeling that everyone is trying to harm you.

phencyclidine (PCP) Hallucinogen that is made in a chemical laboratory.

prescription drug Drug that must be ordered by a doctor.

pusher Drug seller.

snort To take a drug by inhaling or sniffing it.

snuff Form of powdered tobacco that is inhaled, chewed, or placed against the gums.

tar Cancer-causing substance in tobacco.

tetrahydrocannabinol (THC) The main chemical in marijuana.

tolerance Need for more and more of a drug to get the same effect.

tranquilizers Prescription medications that slow the central nervous system.

withdrawal The feeling of anxiety, fear, or confusion when a person stops taking a drug.

For Further Reading

Drugs and You. South Deerfield, MA: Channing L. Bete Co. Inc., 1989.

Drug Use in America. Rockville, MD: U.S. Dept. of Health and Human Services, National Clearinghouse for Alcohol and Drug Information, 1988.

Hurwitz, Sue, and Shniderman, Nancy. *Drugs and Your Friends*. New York: Rosen Publishing Group, 1992.

McFarland, Rhoda. *Coping with Substance Abuse*, rev. ed. New York: Rosen Publishing Group, 1990.

Shapiro, Harry. *Waiting for the Man: The Story of Drugs and Popular Music*. New York: William Morrow & Co., 1988.

Straight Talk about Drugs Means More Than Just Saying No. Weymouth, MA: Life Skills Education.

Index

About the Author

Carlienne Frisch has written books on such diverse topics as pet care, European countries, and the author Maud Hart Lovelace. Before becoming a free-lance writer, she worked as an editor for a farm magazine and in public relations for nonprofit organizations.

The author is president of the Friends of the Minnesota Valley Regional Library and a member of the Society of Children's Book Writers, Habitat for Humanity, and the local historical society. She enjoys reading mysteries and historical novels. She also collects, decorates, and furnishes dollhouses. Ms. Frisch and her husband, Robert, have four adult children. They share their home with York, a tortoise-shell cat.

Photo Credits

Cover photo: © Maje Waldo
Photos on pages 2, 8, 13, 30, 33, 36, 39, 40, 43, 44 © AP/Wide World Photos; all other photos: © Lauren Piperno